Peyton's Magical Hearing Aid

Written by Niki Halwani

Illustrated by TullipStudio

ISBN-13: 979-8-218-14946-8

This book is dedicated to my daughter Peyton who inspired me to write this story.
May you continue to meet adversity head on with the courage and kindness that you display in your everyday life.

May your story serve as inspiration to all hearing-impaired children and their families in realizing that imperfections make you perfect.

I also hope this book promotes awareness among the hearing. Thank you to our family, friends, and the professionals who were involved in helping Peyton.

It was Peyton's first day of kindergarten, and she was so excited to make some new friends.

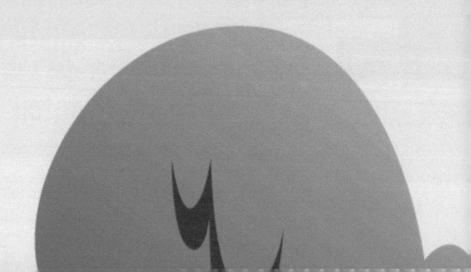

KINDERGARTEN

But everyone in her class asked her the same question...
"What's that in your ear?"

04

So Peyton gathered her new friends around and told them all about how she got her magical hearing aid.

Ever since Peyton was a baby, she loved to sing and dance and watch movies, but she always seemed to turn the volume up very, very loud.

VOLUME

This worried Peyton's Mommy, so she took her to an ear doctor to see if Peyton was having trouble hearing.

And Mommy was right! When the doctor checked Peyton's ears, it seemed like she could only hear out of one.

To find out exactly what was wrong, Peyton went to an ear expert. They played so many fun games together.

Peyton's favorite game involved a bucket and a banana. All she had to do was drop the banana into the bucket whenever she heard a sound.

After the tests with the ear expert, they found that Peyton couldn't hear in her left ear.
That's why she had been struggling to hear the TV!

Fortunately, ear doctors are very clever and knew just what she needed...
Peyton's magical hearing aid!

It looked like an invention from the future, and Peyton thought it was very cool.

They took a mold of her ear and designed a special device just for her.

A couple of weeks later, Peyton returned to the ear expert's office to try on her new hearing aid.

The first time she put it in, she couldn't help but smile and shout, "Mama! I can hear!"

20

On the way home, Peyton heard so many amazing things. She heard the cars beeping their horns. She heard the birds tweeting in the trees.

She heard the people chatting outside the coffee shop.
She heard the dogs barking and having fun in the park.

And she heard her Mama tell her how cool her hearing aid looked!

The hearing aid was so magical that Peyton could even connect it to her tablet to watch movies and do her homework.

28

The only time she took it out was before her tubby every night, but she kept it in a safe place and looked after it until morning.

Peyton loved her hearing aid so much because it let her learn and play with the other kids at school.

32

And once Peyton told her new friends about her magical hearing aid, they all thought it was so cool!

"You're like a real-life superhero!" they cheered.

Peyton was proud of her magical hearing aid. She couldn't wait to get home and tell Mama all about her wonderful first day of kindergarten.

Made in United States
Troutdale, OR
11/11/2024

24688522R00029